Alyssa the Snow Queen Fairy

A gift from the fairies for Amelie Ferguson

ORCHARD BOOKS
Carmelite House, 50 Victoria Embankment, EZ4Y 0DZ
Orchard Books Australia
Level 17/207 Kent Street, Sydney, NSW 2000
A Paperback Original

First published in 2015 by Orchard Books

A CIP catalogue record for this book is available from the British Library.

ISBN 978 1 40833 955 8

1 3 5 7 9 10 8 6 4 2

Printed in Great Britain

The paper and board used in this book are made from wood from responsible sources

Orchard Books is an imprint of Hachette Children's Group and published by the Watts Publishing Group Limited, an Hachette UK company.

www.hachette.co.uk

Alyssa the Snow Queen Fairy

by Daisy Meadows

www.rainbowmagic.co.uk

The Fairyland Palace
Alyssa's Tower
Rachel's House
Tippington Town

Jack Frost's
Ice Castle
Blue Mountains
Tippington Park

Jack Frost's Spell

Wintry weather's my domain.
I love the hail and freezing rain.
Alyssa's magic makes me sneer.
The winter gloom should last all year!

I want the winter winds to bite
And folk to shiver day and night.
I'll steal her icy spells and then
The spring will never come again!

The Magical Snowflake

Contents

Dull December

"What an icy, grey December this is," said Rachel Walker, blowing on her fingers and shivering. "I'm starting to wonder if Christmas will ever arrive!"

It was Saturday morning, and Rachel was in her garden with her best friend, Kirsty Tate. They had come out to play a game of ball, but the sleet was getting heavier. Kirsty shivered too, and buried her hands deep in her pockets.

"I'm really glad to be staying with you for the weekend, but I wish the weather wasn't so horrible," she said.

"We had such lovely things planned," said Rachel. "But nature walks and boating on the lake won't be much fun when it's so miserable and freezing. It looks as if we'll be spending most of the weekend inside."

"Never mind," said Kirsty, grinning at her friend. "We always have fun when we're together, no matter what we're doing."

"You're right," said Rachel, trying to forget about the dark clouds above.

"Perhaps we should go inside," Kirsty

said. "I think it's starting to snow."

"Oh, really?" said Rachel, feeling more cheerful. "Maybe we can go sledging."

"I don't think so," said Kirsty. "I can only see one snowflake."

She pointed up to the single, perfect snowflake. It was spiralling down from the grey sky. The girls watched it land on the edge of a stone birdbath.

"That's funny," said Rachel after a moment. "It's not melting."

Kirsty took a step closer to the birdbath.

"I think it's getting bigger," she said.

The snowflake began to grow bigger and bigger. Then it popped like a snowy balloon and the girls saw a tiny fairy standing in its place. She was as exquisite as the snowflake had been. Her blonde hair flowed around her shoulders, and she was wearing a long blue gown, decorated with sparkling silver sequins.

A furry cape was wrapped around her shoulders, and a snowflake tiara twinkled on her head.

"Hello, Rachel and Kirsty," said the fairy. "I'm Alyssa the Snow Queen Fairy."

"Hello, Alyssa!" said Rachel. "It's great to meet you!"

"What are you doing here in Tippington?" Kirsty asked.

"I've come to ask for your help," said Alyssa in a silvery voice. "It's my job to make sure that everyone stays happy in winter – in both the human and fairy worlds. I went to visit Queen Titania this morning, and when I came home I got a terrible shock. Jack Frost had gone into my home and taken my three magical objects. Without the magical snowflake, the enchanted mirror and the everlasting rose, I can't look after human beings *or* fairies this winter."

"Oh no, that's awful!" Rachel

exclaimed. "Is there any way that we can help you?"

Alyssa clasped her hands together.

"Please, would you come to Fairyland with me?" she asked. "Queen Titania has told me so much about you. When I found that my objects were missing, I thought of you straight away. Will you help me to find out what Jack Frost has done with them?"

Kirsty and Rachel nodded at once.

"Of course we will," Kirsty replied.

"Then let's go!" exclaimed Alyssa, holding up her wand.

The Magical Tower

Glittering snowflakes burst out from Alyssa's wand like a fountain and landed on the girls.

"They're as light as butterfly kisses," said Rachel, laughing.

She and Kirsty had already shrunk to fairy size, and their gossamer wings were fluttering, eager to fly. They felt a cool wind whirl around them, lifting them into the air. They were carried towards the dark clouds with Alyssa at their side.

"I think the world's getting even more gloomy," said Kirsty, looking down.

Sleet was driving down all over Tippington, and the girls felt glad to be leaving the bad weather behind. Better still, they were going to Fairyland!

Rachel and Kirsty were secret friends with the fairies, and they always adored the magical adventures they shared.

Swirling snowflakes surrounded them now, until all they could see was glitter. When the snowflakes cleared, they were standing beside a tall white tower, and they were wrapped in warm fluffy capes, just like the one Alyssa was wearing. All around, as far as they could see, were tall, blue mountains, topped with snow.

"Welcome to my home," said Alyssa, smiling at the girls.

The tower walls were not solid like the walls of the Fairyland Palace. Standing close to them, Rachel and Kirsty saw that they were made of swirling snow.

"That's amazing," said Rachel.

She reached out to touch the wall. It felt cold and coarse.

"But where's the door?" Kirsty asked.

"There is no door," said Alyssa with a laugh. "You just need to trust me."

She took their hands and led them forward.

"We're going to walk into the wall!" Rachel exclaimed.

But she remembered what Alyssa had said, and she kept walking. Instead of hitting the wall, they walked straight through it into Alyssa's home!

It was warm and welcoming, with thick rugs, a roaring fire and big sofas covered in cosy, colourful throws. Hundreds of tiny golden lights were looped around the room. When they looked up, they saw that the tower was hollow, and filled with lights all the way to the roof.

"Why doesn't the fire melt the tower?" Kirsty asked.

"It's a magical fire," Alyssa replied.

"I know spells to make it easy to live in cold weather. I have lived here for a long time, you see."

"Where are we?" asked Rachel.

"We are in the most remote part of Fairyland," said Alyssa. "I live among the Blue Ice Mountains, far beyond Jack Frost's castle. He had no idea that I lived here until this morning. His goblins drove his carriage the wrong way, and he arrived here while I was at the palace. I knew it was him because I

saw goblin footprints in the snow. So he has my magical objects, and now both Fairyland and the human world are in danger."

"What do your magical objects do?" Kirsty asked.

Alyssa waved her wand, and three pictures appeared in the air in front of the girls – a snowflake, a mirror and a rose.

"The magical snowflake makes winter weather just right," she said. "The enchanted mirror helps everyone to see the difference between good and bad. The everlasting rose ensures that new life is still growing underground, and that flowers will appear again each spring. Without them, winter will be miserable for everyone, and my home will start to suffer, just like the rest of Fairyland."

With another wave of her wand, the pictures broke up into tiny pieces and melted away into nothing.

"What do you mean?" asked Rachel.

"Come with me and I will show you," said Alyssa.

She flew upwards and they followed her, higher

and higher, until they passed through the roof and fluttered out among the snow clouds above.

"It's like flying through cotton wool," said Kirsty with a giggle.

Alyssa led the way and the girls sped after her. Suddenly there was a break in the clouds, and they saw that the Ice Castle was directly below them. They were flying in the direction of the Fairyland Palace!

Winter in Fairyland

As they flew closer to the palace, the snow clouds separated a little. Rachel and Kirsty gazed down in surprise. They had been to Fairyland in winter before and they knew how snowy and beautiful it usually looked. But today the snow was streaked with mud. It looked hard and icy instead of soft and powdery. There were no fairies playing outside at all, and icicles hung from their toadstool houses.

"I don't understand," said Rachel. "Why is the snow so dirty?"

"It's bitterly cold," Kirsty said. "There's hail in the wind."

"It feels like needles on my face," said Rachel.

Alyssa stopped and fluttered above a frozen pond. She looked worried and upset.

"This is happening because my magical snowflake is missing," she said. "You see, it makes wintry weather

beautiful and calm, and never too harsh or too cold. I share that magic across the human and fairy worlds, but Jack Frost has taken it all for himself. Now everyone else will suffer. Jack Frost's home will have pleasant, snowy winter weather, but Fairyland and the human world will have nothing but grey skies, solid ice and muddy snow."

"That's really strange," said Kirsty. "Jack Frost loves the ice and cold. Why would he want his home to be softer and more snowy?"

"I think we should go to the

Ice Castle and try to find out," said Rachel.

Alyssa nodded.

"I hope that he is keeping my magical objects there," she said. "Do you think we can find them?"

"Of course we can," said Rachel. "We just have to find out what he's planning – and stop him!"

It was strange for the weather to get better when they reached the Ice Castle. Fat snowflakes were floating down over the castle, and when the fairies flew over the battlements, they saw goblin guards building snowmen.

"Look down there," said Rachel, pointing to a lawn in the castle gardens. A large group of goblins was gathered, sitting on garden chairs and swinging their legs. The chairs were facing a small bandstand, where Jack Frost was sitting on a throne of ice.

"You've found him!" Alyssa said. "Well done!"

Rachel, Kirsty and Alyssa fluttered to the ground and crouched down behind a hedge. Peeping around, they could see that Jack Frost had a book in his hands, from which he seemed to be reading aloud. Beside him was a table, and on the table was a domed glass case.

"Look!" said Alyssa in an excited whisper. "Look inside the glass case!"

Rachel and Kirsty looked, and saw a single snowflake floating magically in the middle of the dome. It was perfect in every detail.

"Is that your magical snowflake?" asked Kirsty. "It's beautiful!"

"We've found it!" said Rachel, giving a little hop of triumph.

"Yes," said Alyssa, her face falling. "But how are we going to get it back in front of all these goblins?"

The Snow Queen Appears

The three fairies thought for a moment, but they couldn't think of a single idea. They looked around at the goblins. Some of them were listening to their master, but most were fidgeting and whispering to each other.

"What is Jack Frost reading to those goblins?" Kirsty asked.

They strained to hear, and then caught a few words drifting towards them. "Gerda and Kay heard the church bells ringing and knew that they were home."

"I know that story!" Rachel exclaimed. "It's *The Snow Queen* – my mum always reads it to me at Christmas. But why is he reading it to the goblins?"

Just then the story ended, and Jack Frost turned to the front of the book again. The fairies saw two of the nearest goblins fidget and lean towards each other.

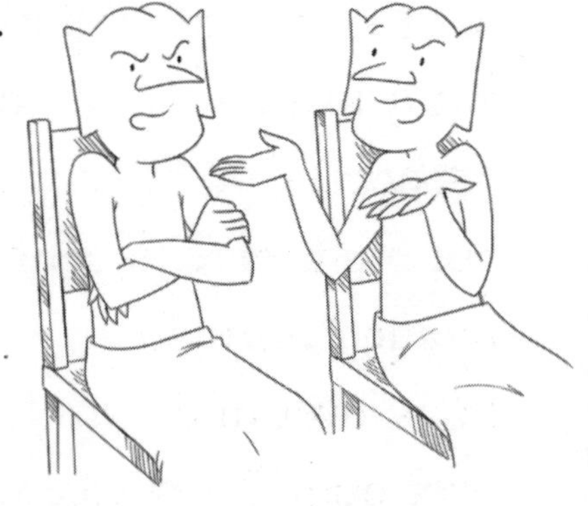

"He's going to read it again," said one with a groan.

"We've already had to listen to it

three times," grumbled the other. "I wish somebody would stop him!"

Just then, a goblin closer to Jack Frost stood up.

"Er, can we have a different story this time?" he asked. "I'm bored of that one."

"Boring! Boring!" chanted a few of the other goblins.

"Shut up!" Jack Frost snarled at them. "I'm the boss, so you have to do what I say."

"What's the point of reading a stupid book over and over again?" asked another goblin. "And who cares about the Snow Queen anyway?"

"You numbskulls!" Jack Frost shrieked. "You nitwits!"

He almost threw the book at the goblin who was standing up, and then thought better of it.

"You need to learn about the Snow Queen," he said through gritted teeth, "because she'll be giving you orders very soon. She will rule everything with me, as soon as she sees that my powerful magic has turned everywhere else to ice. Together we will rule both Fairyland and the human world! She is the only one who can enjoy the cold as I can, so obviously she's going to want to find me. I am going to read about her until she arrives, and you will listen, like it or not."

"He doesn't know that *The Snow Queen* is a fairy tale," said Kirsty. "He thinks that there is a real Snow Queen – and he wants to rule the world with her!"

"*That's* why he's taken the snowflake," said Rachel. "He has used all its magic to make the Ice Castle snowy and beautiful, so that everywhere else is turned to ice."

As Jack Frost started reading the story again, Kirsty clasped her hands together and turned to Rachel and Alyssa.

"I've got it!" she whispered. "Alyssa, could you make a snow queen out of ice? Something that could fool Jack Frost?"

"Certainly," said Alyssa.

She flicked her wand, and a ribbon of ice shot out of the tip. In a few seconds, it had built up into an ice statue of a beautiful woman. She looked proud and haughty, and she wore a high crown and a set of flowing robes.

She was very beautiful, and she had one hand raised as if she were waving.

The statue stood at the back of the crowd of goblins, so it was a few moments before Jack Frost spotted it.

He stopped reading at once, and jumped to his feet, waving one hand and smoothing down his beard with the other.

"Welcome, Your Majesty!" he said in a grovelling voice. "I am honoured to see you in my icy domain."

The goblins turned around and let out squawks of excitement.

"The Snow Queen is here!"

"I want her autograph!"

"What's she wearing?"

"I want to shake her hand!"

They leaped towards the model, and Jack Frost sprang after them.

"Don't crowd her!" he bellowed. "Show some respect!"

"Now's our chance!" said Kirsty.

While the goblins and Jack Frost had their backs turned, she and Rachel zoomed over to rescue the magical snowflake. But as they lifted the glass dome, an

unlucky puff of wind sent the snowflake dancing through the air – straight towards Jack Frost!

Spinning Snowflake

"No!" cried Alyssa.

She flew out from her hiding place, and the goblins and Jack Frost saw her.

For a brief moment, no one moved. Jack Frost stared first at Alyssa, then at Rachel and Kirsty, and then at the Snow Queen ice statue.

"What?" he stammered. "Who… how…?"

Another puff of wind made the magical snowflake spin faster, and it seemed to shake Jack Frost out of his surprise.

"Get that snowflake NOW!" he roared.

The goblins flung themselves forward across the powdery snow, their arms stretched out to catch the snowflake. Several of them fell flat on their faces and sank into the snow. Some went in too deep and got stuck. Not one of them could lay his hands on the slippery snowflake.

Rachel and Kirsty darted towards the snowflake too, zigzagging around the capering goblins. The snowflake danced above them, pushed this way and that by all the hands flapping towards it. Then

the girls heard an outraged screech and turned to see Jack Frost holding the hand of the Snow Queen statue. He had tried to shake her hand and then realised that she was made of ice!

"I'll teach you to try to trick me!" he shouted, glaring at Alyssa. "I'll make sure you've lost all your magical objects for ever!"

"I will not let you selfishly spoil winter for everyone," Alyssa declared.

"My goblins outnumber you three pests," Jack Frost cackled. "Any moment now they will catch your magical snowflake and it will be mine!"

"That's never going to happen!" Rachel exclaimed.

Just then a goblin actually touched the snowflake. He batted it towards Jack Frost, who laughed and reached out to catch it. But one more puff of wind lifted it above his head, a little out of arm's reach. Still laughing, Jack Frost rose on his tiptoes, but this time the puff of wind was lucky. The snowflake was blown away from the Ice Lord…and straight into Alyssa's arms!

"Hurray!" shouted Rachel and Kirsty, as Alyssa twirled upwards, clutching the snowflake to her chest and laughing happily. Below, Jack Frost shouted and stamped in fury. He kicked the statue and then hopped around, clutching his toe and shouting.

Rachel and Kirsty flew up beside Alyssa as the snow in Jack Frost's garden grew icy again, and new icicles appeared on the castle.

"Look," said Alyssa, pointing at the distant hills of Fairyland.

The muddy snow had turned to brilliant white, and they could see that some of the fairies had come outside to start a friendly snowball fight.

"It's a proper Fairyland winter again," said Kirsty with relief. "Thank goodness!"

"It's all thanks to you and Rachel," said Alyssa. "I will return my magical snowflake to my tower and send you both home."

"But what about your other magical objects?" Rachel asked. "We want to help you find them too."

"Thank you, my dear friends," said Alyssa, smiling at them. "That would be wonderful. I will come and fetch you again soon. But for now, goodbye!"

She waved her wand, and everything around the girls began to shimmer.

A few seconds later, they were standing once more in Rachel's garden.

"What an exciting adventure!" said Kirsty, sounding a little breathless.

"The grey clouds are scudding away," said Rachel, looking up. "The sun's coming out too. We did it, Kirsty!"

The girls held hands and spun around in the winter sunshine.

"We just have to be ready to find the other magical objects," Kirsty said. "Jack Frost still has the enchanted mirror and the everlasting rose."

"We'll help Alyssa to get them back," said Rachel. "And I can't wait to see her again!"

The Enchanted Mirror

Contents

A Frosty Night

"It's another chilly evening," said Mr Walker. "Let's light the fire."

Night had fallen, and a cold wind was rattling the windows of the Walkers' house. Rachel and Kirsty were curled up on the sofa with Buttons the dog between them. They watched Mr Walker kneel down beside the fire and scrunch up some newspaper, make a pyramid of sticks and add a few lumps of coal.

Soon, orange flames were leaping up from the grate, and the girls were feeling snug and sleepy. They sipped the warm milk that Mrs Walker had made and smiled at each other. It had been a wonderful day. They had met Alyssa the Snow Queen Fairy and helped her to rescue the magical snowflake from Jack Frost. Best of all, they felt sure that more adventures were on the way.

"This is what I love about winter," said Kirsty as the fire crackled. "Snuggling up beside a cosy fire makes up for all the cold weather."

Mrs Walker glanced at the clock on the mantelpiece.

"Girls, don't go upstairs and get ready for bed," she said. "It's important that you get as little sleep as possible so that you will be too tired to play tomorrow."

Rachel and Kirsty looked up, feeling confused.

"Don't you mean that you *want* us to go to bed?" Rachel asked.

Mrs Walker shook her head as if she had been daydreaming.

"Of course you need to go to bed," she said with a puzzled expression. "I made a mistake."

Kirsty and Rachel made their way upstairs, feeling a bit unsettled. As they were getting into their pyjamas, Kirsty frowned.

"That was an odd mistake for your mum to make," she said. "Do you think it could have anything to do with Alyssa's magic mirror being missing?"

"Why do you think that?" Rachel asked.

"Alyssa said it helps people think and see clearly," said Kirsty. "Perhaps now that Jack Frost has it, everybody is getting confused."

Before Rachel could reply, the girls heard a tinkling noise. Then there was a faint tapping at the window, and they both jumped.

"Quickly, open the curtains!" said Rachel, feeling excited. "I think that might be magic!"

Together, the girls drew open the curtains.

The window was covered in frost, in the most beautiful patterns they had ever seen. There were loops and swirls, delicate flowers and sparkling stars. Through a snowflake shape, they saw a tiny, beautiful face peeping at them and waving.

It was Alyssa!

Rachel opened the window and Alyssa fluttered inside. Her long blue gown was sparkling with frost as well as sequins.

"It's lovely to see you, Alyssa!" said Kirsty. "But why are you out on such a bitterly cold night?"

"I'm here to ask for your help again," said Alyssa. "Things are bad in the human world...and even worse in Fairyland."

"Is it because of your missing mirror?" Rachel asked.

Alyssa nodded, tears glistening on her tiny eyelashes.

"People and fairies are getting confused between good and bad," she said.

"Rachel's mum got confused about bedtime earlier," said Kirsty.

"It will get worse as long as Jack Frost has my enchanted mirror," said Alyssa. "Some of the fairies are in danger already."

"What do you mean?" asked Rachel in alarm.

"Jack Frost is angry with me because I fooled him with the Snow Queen statue," Alyssa explained. "He has used my enchanted mirror to trick some of the young fairies from the Fairyland School. He has made them go to work for him in his home."

Rachel and Kirsty were horrified.

"Fairies working in the Ice Castle?" said Kirsty. "We have to do something to help them!"

"Come to Fairyland with me now," Alyssa said, stretching her arms wide. "Together we must stop Jack Frost and his mischievous plans!"

Fairies in Danger

Alyssa raised her wand and smiled. Instantly, they felt warm all over, as if a cloak had been wrapped around them. They looked down and saw that they were shrinking to fairy size. Alyssa had given each of them a long, fluffy coat with a snuggly hood, and their fairy wings were fluttering on their backs.

Just then, they heard footsteps on the stairs outside.

"It's Mum!" said Rachel. "She's coming to say goodnight – we have to go before she sees us."

"Don't worry," said Alyssa, lifting her wand again. "Remember, while you're in Fairyland, time stands still in the human world. And my magic will take you to Fairyland in the blink of an eye!"

And as the girls blinked, they were whooshed off their feet and twirled around in the air. Their heads spinning, they opened their eyes and found themselves standing on the battlements of the Ice Castle. Stars were glittering above, lighting up two goblin guards who were pacing towards them.

"Quick, hide!" Alyssa whispered.

They darted behind a turret just in time. The goblin guards walked right up to it and paused.

"I don't like the night shift," said the tallest goblin. "It's too cold."

"You're just scared of the dark," said the second goblin with a snigger.

"Am not!" the tallest goblin shouted. "You're the one who ran away from your own shadow last week!"

Two more goblin guards appeared out of the gloom.

"Hey, you two lazybones," said one of them. "Why aren't you marching up and down?"

"It's too chilly for marching," said the tallest goblin.

"It's too chilly to be outside at all," said one of the others.

Behind the turret, Rachel had an idea. She whispered in Alyssa's ear, and the Snow Queen Fairy nodded. She waved her wand and whispered,

"Winter treats for goblins four!
Snacks to eat and drinks to pour.
Let them guzzle, gulp and gobble.
We'll sneak inside while they all squabble!"

A single sparkle of fairy dust came dancing out of her wand and looped the loop

towards the goblins. It hit the ground in front of them with a bang, and instantly a camping stool appeared with four sheepskin-lined chairs. On the table were four woolly Balaclavas, four mugs of creamy, bubbling hot chocolate and a tin of marshmallows. On the side of the box, in ice-blue writing, were the words, 'Love from Jack Frost'.

"Hurray!" shouted the tallest goblin. "Jack Frost is the *best*!"

Rachel clapped her hands together in delight as the goblins hurried over to the table. Soon, all four of them were slurping the hot chocolate and cramming marshmallows into their mouths. They were so busy enjoying the treats that they didn't notice the fairies flutter past them. Rachel, Kirsty and Alyssa landed in front of the door that led from the battlements into the castle. It was locked and bolted.

"What shall we do?" asked Kirsty with a groan.

"We won't let a little thing like a locked door stop us," said Alyssa with a sudden grin.

She lightly touched the padlock on the door with her wand, and it sprang open. The chain dropped to the floor with a crash, and Rachel and Kirsty glanced around at the goblins, worried that they might have heard.

"Don't worry about them," said Alyssa. "Those Balaclavas are magic – they stop the wearer from hearing anything."

The door swung open and they flew in, listening out for any signs of Jack Frost. Sure enough, they could hear a loud, angry voice from further in the castle.

"It's Jack Frost," said Rachel. "I'd know that voice anywhere."

"You fairies need to work harder!" they

heard Jack Frost shout. "No stopping! No resting! Clean this castle from top to bottom!"

Rachel, Kirsty and Alyssa exchanged determined glances. They had to save the fairies!

Bewitched!

Rachel, Kirsty and Alyssa zoomed along dirty corridors and down damp stairwells, as Jack Frost's yells echoed around them.

"Which way is he?" asked Alyssa, covering her ears. "The noise seems to be coming from all directions at once!"

"That way, I think!" said Kirsty,

pointing along a wide corridor. "It leads to the Throne Room."

They flew a little further along, and stopped when they came to a corner. The shouting was very loud now. They peeped around and saw five young fairies on their hands and knees in the corridor, scrubbing the floor. Jack Frost was watching them with his arms folded.

"Faster!" he shouted. "I want to be able

to see my face shining in this floor when I get back!"

He turned and strode away, his cloak billowing out around him.

"Look at the pocket of his cloak!" said Rachel.

Five fairy wands were sticking out of his pocket.

"He's taken their wands!" Kirsty said in a horrified whisper.

Alyssa darted around the corner and

flew over to the nearest fairy.

"We're here to rescue you," she said. "Come with us!"

But the little fairy shook her head.

"I'm happy here," she said. "This is really good fun."

Rachel and Kirsty fluttered over to stand beside another fairy.

"You're shivering," said Rachel. "You must be freezing. Come with us and Alyssa will use her special magic to warm you up."

"Oh no, I love the cold," said the fairy,

her teeth chattering. "Please, leave us here. We want to stay with Jack Frost. He's so nice to us."

She tried to smile, but her eyes were full of tears and seemed to be pleading with the girls. She looked very confused.

"It's as if they're saying the opposite of how they really feel," said Kirsty.

"They are," said Alyssa in a serious voice, gazing into the fairy's eyes. "Try to remember," she said. "Did Jack Frost make you look into a mirror?"

The fairy nodded, then shook her head,

then nodded again.

"Why would they agree to come here with him?" Kirsty wondered.

"They are very young fairies, and Jack Frost has used the enchanted mirror to confuse and bewitch them," said Alyssa. "They won't see him clearly until the enchanted mirror is back where it belongs – with me!"

"We have to help them," said Rachel. "I can't bear to see them doing such horrible work for Jack Frost."

"Until I have my mirror back, no one in the human or fairy worlds will be able to tell the difference between good and bad," said Alyssa. "The fairies will not want to leave the Ice Castle. To help them, we have to find Jack Frost and take back my mirror!"

It felt awful leaving the five fairies scrubbing the floor, but they had to catch up with Jack Frost. They flew as fast as they could, and glimpsed him just outside the Throne Room. Kirsty looked at the wands in his pocket and frowned.

"There is something else in his pocket with the wands," she said.

"I can see a silver handle," Rachel added, as Jack Frost went through the door.

"My enchanted mirror has a silver handle," said Alyssa.

"Perhaps we've found it!"

They zoomed after him and darted through the door just before it closed. Jack Frost was sitting bolt upright on his throne, glaring at three young fairies who were hovering in front of him. Their hands were clasped behind them and there were no goblins to be seen. Rachel, Kirsty and Alyssa slipped out of sight behind a long curtain.

"I want your wands," Jack Frost was saying to the fairies, holding out his hand. "Give them to me now!"

The fairies did as they were told, and Jack Frost shoved the wands into his pocket. As he did so, Alyssa saw the silver handle and nodded.

"That's my enchanted mirror!" she whispered.

Turning Up the Heat

"You are my new servants," Jack Frost told the young fairies. "I'm fed up with goblins. I want one of you to get a pen and some paper – I'm going to write a book about how I defeated you lot and took over Fairyland. Write down everything I say, and don't miss a single word or you'll be in big trouble!"

The smallest fairy curtsied and found a pen and a piece of paper.

"I'm ready, sir," she said.

"Once, a lot of pesky fairies ruled Fairyland," Jack Frost began. "But then something wonderful happened. Me! With my amazing magic I controlled all the fairies and told them what to do. Here's how I did it…"

"He's so interested in the sound of his own voice, he might not notice if I take the mirror," Kirsty whispered.

"Be careful!" Alyssa exclaimed.

Kirsty nodded, and fluttered over to stand behind the throne. Rachel and Alyssa watched and held their breath as Kirsty reached out her hand. She was almost touching the handle of the enchanted mirror!

Jack Frost shivered and pulled his cloak tightly around him. Now the pocket was out of Kirsty's reach. She flew back behind the curtain and Rachel squeezed her hand.

"Maybe if the room were warmer, he would take off his cloak," she said.

"Could you make it warmer in here, Alyssa?" Kirsty asked.

Alyssa flourished her wand and shimmering hot air streamed out of it, coiling and swirling around the room. Jack Frost was so busy talking

about himself, he didn't notice that the throne room was getting warmer … and warmer … and warmer.

"I don't like to boast," Jack Frost was saying, "but I have the biggest brain in the whole universe, and it was only a matter of time before I found a way to take over from Queen Titania and King Oberon."

His cloak fell open and then slipped to the floor behind the throne.

"Now!" Alyssa whispered.

They darted over to the cloak and shook it, searching for the pocket. But the wands fell out, clicking against each other. The girls heard the sound of someone sucking air in between their teeth, and looked up. Jack Frost was leaning over the back of his throne and glaring at them.

"Thieves!" he yelled.

He leaped over the back of the throne.

Rachel and Alyssa zoomed up out of his reach, but Kirsty wasn't quick enough. As she flew upwards, he grabbed her arm in one bony hand and his cloak in the other. Kirsty was dragged down.

"Let me go!" she cried, struggling against him.

"Release my friend at once!" Alyssa demanded.

"No chance," said Jack Frost. "She's my prisoner now!"

The three young fairies were staring in shock, but none of them moved to help.

Rachel clenched her fists. She had to help her best friend! Suddenly she had an idea.

"Kirsty, listen to me," she said in a loud voice. "Don't be scared – Jack Frost is a coward."

"What do you mean?" Kirsty asked.

"How dare you?" roared Jack Frost.

"He hasn't even dared to take the enchanted mirror out of his pocket," said Rachel with a laugh. "He's probably too scared to look in it!"

"I'm not scared of anything!" bellowed the Ice Lord. "I'll show you!"

Still holding Kirsty with one hand, he managed to pull the mirror out of his cloak pocket. The cloak dropped to the floor, and Jack Frost gazed into the mirror.

At once, a confused look passed over his face. He frowned, and shook his head a couple of times as if he felt dizzy.

Bad is Good!

"Are you sure you want to hold on to Kirsty?" Alyssa asked Jack Frost.

"No way!" he said. He let go of Kirsty's arm, and she flew up to join Rachel and Alyssa.

"He's getting confused between good and bad," Alyssa whispered to the girls.

"That's great for us, because everything Jack Frost thinks is bad, we think is good!"

"Right," said Rachel in a determined voice. "Now I have a question for you, Jack Frost. Is it a good thing or a bad thing to give the enchanted mirror back to Alyssa?"

"It's a good thing!" said Jack Frost in a puzzled voice.

Smiling, Alyssa floated down and held out her hand. Jack Frost handed her

the mirror at once, although there was confusion in his eyes.

As soon as the mirror was in Alyssa's hand, she held it up and cried out,

"Return all thoughts from wrong to
right.
Correct the errors made tonight.
Winter winds bring ice and snow,
But stop Jack Frost
from bringing
woe."

The mirror gave a blue flash that lit up the whole room, and instantly

the confusion left Jack Frost's eyes. The young fairies looked at each other in astonishment. Then the door burst open and the five other fairies darted in.

"Fly up!" Alyssa called out, flinging the cloak over Jack Frost's head.

She seized the wands that had fallen

to the floor and threw them to the fairies. Everyone shot upwards, and Jack Frost capered around in fury, trying to tug the cloak off his head.

"You tricksy fairy!" he bellowed. "I'll make you sorry for this!"

With a flick of Alyssa's wand, the young fairies disappeared.

"I've sent them back to the Fairyland School, where they belong," she told the girls with a smile. "You must go home too, but I promise to see you very soon!"

"You will never find the everlasting rose!" Jack Frost shrieked, dragging the cloak from his head and stamping on it. "My goblins have hidden it, and winter will last forever!"

"With my friends beside me, I can do anything!" Alyssa declared.

She waved her wand again, and Rachel and Kirsty were caught up in a whirl of fairy dust as Alyssa's magic whisked them home. They landed softly on their beds in Rachel's bedroom.

"Goodness, what an adventure!" said Rachel, still a little out of breath.

"My head is still whirling!" Kirsty added with a laugh.

As usual, no time had passed since the girls had gone to Fairyland. Mrs Walker's footsteps reached the top of the stairs, and the bedroom door opened.

"Goodnight, girls," she said with a smile. "Sweet dreams!"

Rachel and Kirsty exchanged a secret smile. They knew that no dreams could be better than the adventure they had just shared!

The Everlasting Rose

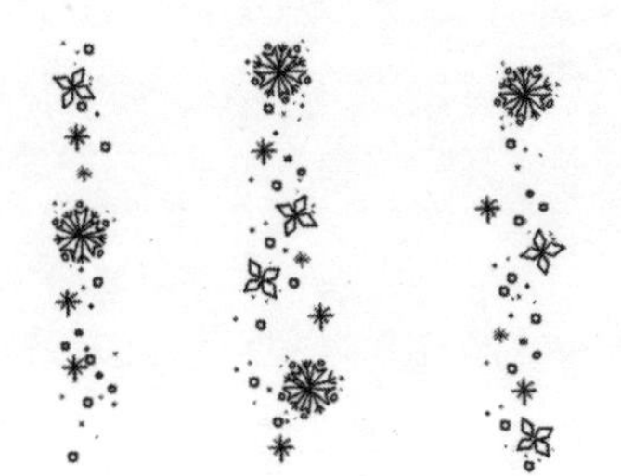

Contents

Devious Divers

"I wish you didn't have to go home later," said Rachel, squeezing Kirsty's hand as they walked along. "I love it when you come to stay."

Kirsty smiled at her. The girls were in the park, giving Buttons his morning walk. He was running back and forwards, sniffing everything and wagging his tail.

"It's been a really magical visit so far," said Kirsty, as Buttons ran over to an empty flowerbed. "Meeting Alyssa was amazing."

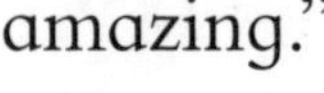

"Yes, it was," Rachel said, remembering Alyssa's enchanted home. "I just hope we can help her to find her third missing magical object."

"The everlasting rose," said Kirsty, nodding. "It sounds beautiful."

Rachel sighed as she looked at the flowerbeds that Buttons was sniffing.

"Without it, these flowerbeds will stay empty," she said. "Alyssa said that her rose makes sure that new life is ready to burst out of the ground when spring comes. Winter will never end if we don't find it."

"That would ruin the cycle of the seasons," said Kirsty. "Every year is supposed to have spring, summer, autumn and winter. If it were winter all the time, people and animals would get ill, and plants wouldn't grow."

Rachel looked at the people in the park. Everyone looked pale, and no one was smiling. A couple of boys were walking away from the lake, carrying fishing rods.

"We can't fish when the lake is frozen over," the girls heard one of them say. "I don't like winter."

"Oh no," said Rachel, feeling sad. "Winter is a beautiful season, but no one wants a season to last for ever. People will start to dislike it!"

At that moment they were walking towards a large bush, thick with frost. As they drew level with it, they both heard a squeaky, echoing giggle. They stopped and stared at each other.

"Could that be …?" said Kirsty.

"It sounded like …" said Rachel.

"GOBLINS!" they exclaimed together.

They crouched down and peered under the bush. A few feet away, at the hollow centre of the bush, were three very strange figures indeed. They were wearing green diving suits with round, glass diving helmets.

"You sound really weird!" one of them was yelling.

His voice echoed as if he were shouting in a tunnel. The others giggled and bashed their helmets together.

"You look like green goldfish in a bowl!" another goblin hooted, pointing at the other two and laughing.

"Well you look like a nincompoop," snapped the third goblin. "And you'll *still* look like an idiot when you take the diving suit off, so there!"

The goblins lowered their voices.

"We have to get closer," Kirsty whispered. "They might know something about the everlasting rose."

The girls crawled a little way into the bush as quietly as they could. Now they could hear what the goblins were saying. And just then, they heard something that made them stare at each other in excitement.

"This time Jack Frost has thought of the best hiding place ever," the first goblin said. "There is no way that those pesky, goody-two-shoes fairies can get to the bottom of a frozen lake. Not even Alyssa the Snow Queen Fairy!"

Rachel and Kirsty shared a smile.

"Now we know exactly where to find the rose!" Kirsty whispered.

"Not *exactly*," Rachel replied. "The lake is really big. We have to know where to look."

Suddenly there was a volley of barks and Buttons came bounding into the bush.

"Buttons, no!" Rachel whispered.

But Buttons had seen goblins before. If there was one thing he knew, it was that goblins were naughty, and he should get rid of them as quickly as possible.

"Run!" the goblins howled as Buttons charged towards them. "Protect the rose!"

Alyssa Appears

Rachel managed to grab Buttons by the collar. She clipped on his lead and hugged him, shaking her head.

"Oh Buttons, I know you think you're helping," she said. "But now the goblins will know that we are trying to get the rose back."

She led the panting dog out of the bush, followed by Kirsty. The girls scrambled to their feet.

"Come on!" said Kirsty, grabbing Rachel's hand. "We've got to stop one of those goblins and make him show us where the rose is hidden!"

Rachel and Kirsty sprinted towards the lake, with Buttons bounding along beside them. He thought it was a jolly game, and was joining in with enthusiasm. He didn't understand everything about goblins and fairies, but he knew one thing: Whenever Rachel and Kirsty were together, there were always great adventures to be had!

They skidded to a halt at the edge of the ice-crusted lake, and looked around. Then Rachel let out a cry and pointed to the bank opposite. The three goblins were standing in a line, jostling with each other to get in front. There was a large, round hole in the ice in front of them. As the girls watched, the goblins jumped through the hole one by one and disappeared into the deep lake.

Kirsty

groaned. "We can't follow them in there! What are we going to do?"

"I have no idea," said Rachel, biting her lip. "Hey – what's that?"

A small speck was whizzing towards them across the lake.

"Is it Alyssa?" Kirsty asked, her hopes rising.

"No, it's a bird," said Rachel. "I've never seen one like it before, though."

Kirsty peered at the bird as it flew towards them.

"Wow, I wish my dad could see this," she said. "He loves birds, and that's a really unusual one. I've only ever seen a picture of it in his bird book. It's called a snow bunting because of its white feathers."

"It's coming straight towards us," said

Rachel, feeling a little nervous. "Do snow buntings *like* humans?"

"It's going to crash into us!" Kirsty cried. "Duck!"

The girls dropped to the ground, and Buttons hid his head under his paws. But

when the snow bunting reached the bank where they were standing, it slowed down and landed on the lake edge. Rachel and Kirsty smiled and stood up, for sitting on the bird's back was the beautiful Snow Queen Fairy.

"Alyssa!" they shouted together.

"Thank goodness you're here," Rachel added. "We know where the everlasting rose is!"

Alyssa gave a delighted gasp and slipped off the back of the snow bunting. Her sparkling blue gown swirled around her as she kissed the bird.

"Thank you for bringing me here," she said. "You fly much faster than I do, my little friend."

The snow bunting twittered a goodbye and flew away across the park.

"Now, tell me everything," said Alyssa.

She fluttered upwards and hovered in front of the girls. Luckily it was so cold that no one was walking around the lake, so there was no danger of her being seen.

"We saw three goblins wearing diving suits," Kirsty explained. "They were talking about how clever Jack Frost had been to hide the everlasting rose at the bottom of this lake."

"But the goblins saw us, and ran off," Rachel continued. "So we followed them here and watched them jump into the lake through that hole. They've gone to guard the rose."

She pointed at the hole, and Alyssa zoomed upwards to see it properly. When she floated back down, she was looking very upset.

"I can't fly underwater," she said. "Oh girls, I think Jack Frost has defeated me!"

Sparkling Skates

The girls could see that Alyssa was starting to give up hope. Her shoulders slumped and she gazed down at the ground. Suddenly, Rachel thought of the boys they had seen earlier, carrying their fishing rods home.

"We can't go underwater," she said, "but perhaps we could fish for the rose.

Alyssa, could you magic up a fishing rod for us?"

"I could," said Alyssa, looking puzzled. "But if the goblins are guarding the rose, they can easily stop us from hooking it with a fishing rod."

"That's true," said Kirsty. "We'll have to get them out of the way somehow. We're not going to let Jack Frost win, Alyssa!"

"You're right," Alyssa replied. "With my magic and your wonderful ideas, we are unbeatable. We just need to think of something that will be more interesting to the goblins than guarding the rose."

Kirsty and Rachel exchanged amused glances. They knew the answer to this question.

"Snacks!" they said together.

All goblins loved snacks, and usually

found them impossible to resist. Alyssa waved her wand, and three clear plastic snack boxes appeared on the ground beside her. They each contained a green cupcake, a packet of green biscuits, a bag of green, stripy sweets, some green jelly babies and a bag of goblin-shaped crisps. On the side of each box were the words 'DO NOT OPEN UNDERWATER'.

"Perfect!" exclaimed Rachel, clapping her hands together.

Alyssa gave another little flick of her wand,

and a fishing rod appeared in Kirsty's hand. Rachel picked up the snack boxes and looked across at the hole.

"It's going to take us ages to walk around the lake to the other side," she said.

But Alyssa smiled. She raised her wand for a third time and recited a spell.

"Come snow, come ice, do not delay,
Or cruel Jack Frost will win the day.
Help me now, for winter's sake,
And speed my friends across the lake."

Instantly, both of the girls realised they were wearing a pair of glittering skates.

"They are made of ice," said Alyssa with a smile. "They will last just long enough to get you to the other side of the lake, and then they will melt away."

"Wait here, Buttons," said Rachel.

Buttons lay down again, and then Kirsty and Rachel stepped onto the ice, feeling nervous and excited at the same time. But they needn't have worried. The skates were perfectly shaped for their feet, and soon they were gliding across the frozen lake, striking out towards the hole where the goblins had disappeared.

"This is so much fun!" Kirsty exclaimed happily.

Even though they were worried about the everlasting rose, both girls were thrilled by the *swish-swish* of their magical skates on the ice, and the cold wind on their cheeks. The wonderful journey was over too quickly, and soon they were stepping onto the bank on the other side. Alyssa had flown ahead, and was already waiting for them there.

"That was wonderful," said Rachel in a breathless voice.

As she spoke, her ice skates melted away into nothing. Kirsty's did the same.

"I'm glad you enjoyed it," said Alyssa. "Skating is one of the most enchanting things about winter."

Rachel took the end of the fishing line and hooked it onto one of the snack boxes. Then Kirsty carried the fishing rod over to the hole in the ice. She dropped the box into the freezing water and let it sink downwards.

"I think it's reached the bottom," she said after a few moments. "Oh! Something is tugging on the line!"

A Fishing Trip

Kirsty turned the reel handle, and the fishing rod bent as it pulled on something heavy.

"It's coming!" said Kirsty.

Then, with a splash and spray of water, one of the goblins shot out through the hole and landed on the bank. He was clinging to the snack box, and as the girls watched he tore off his helmet, opened the box and started to munch on the food. Then he noticed Alyssa, Rachel and Kirsty, and his eyes opened wide. His mouth was so full that he couldn't say a word.

"Home you go!" Alyssa sang out.

She waved her wand, and the goblin vanished in a flurry of sparkling snowflakes.

"One down, two to go," said Rachel. "Time to go fishing again, Kirsty!"

The second snack box went underwater, and exactly the same thing happened. The second goblin was sent back home, still munching his snacks. Kirsty sent the third box down through the hole, and soon the fishing rod started to bend again.

"I've got him," she said. "As soon as he is safely out of the way, we can fish for the everlasting rose."

But this time, when the goblin came shooting out of the water, he wasn't just holding a snack box. Tucked under his other arm was a sealed glass box, and inside the box was the most beautiful rose that the girls had ever seen. Its velvety petals were deep red, and there were drops of dew clinging to its delicate leaves. It looked as if it had just been picked.

"My rose!" Alyssa exclaimed.

Her voice sounded loving and worried at the same time. The goblin pulled off his helmet, stuffed half the cupcake into his mouth and gave them all an unpleasant grin.

"I knew there was some fairy trickery going on," he said, spraying cupcake crumbs everywhere.

"It's rude to talk with your mouth full," said Kirsty. "Almost as rude as taking Alyssa's belongings."

The goblin ignored her. He was far too busy feeling pleased with himself.

"I'm so clever!" he boasted. "I guessed that one of those pesky fairies was sending the snacks down, but I was the only goblin who thought of a way to keep the rose safe *and* eat my snacks!"

"Give the rose back to Alyssa," said Rachel. "It doesn't belong to you."

"Are you kidding?" asked the goblin in an impertinent tone. "I'm taking the rose straight back to Jack Frost, so he can see how wonderful I am. Then he'll choose another hiding place – one that you will *never* find!"

Suddenly, Kirsty remembered Jack Frost reading *The Snow Queen* to the goblins. She thought of the puzzle that the Snow Queen used to keep little Kay a prisoner, and that gave her an idea.

"You're right," she said. "You have been very clever. You've been too clever for us – we never thought that you might take the everlasting rose away with you."

The goblin puffed out his chest, and Alyssa looked at Kirsty in surprise. But Rachel smiled – she could always tell when her best friend had a plan!

"Before you go, we have something that you might find interesting," Kirsty went on. "It's an ice puzzle, but only someone who is really, really clever will be able to complete it. Would you like to give it a try?"

She winked at Alyssa, who was holding her wand behind her back. She gave it a little shake, and there was a tinkling sound like falling glass. Nine large pieces of ice thumped onto the ground in front of the goblin.

"It's a magical ice jigsaw," Alyssa explained. "The pieces look blank now, but when they are all fitted together, your face will appear on the puzzle."

Looking excited, the goblin started to try to fit the pieces together. But he kept dropping them because his arms were so full.

"Perhaps you should put the snack box down," Rachel suggested.

Nodding, the goblin laid the snack box down beside him. But it was very difficult to hold on to the large pieces of ice with just one hand.

"Bother!" he squawked as another one slipped out of his grasp.

"You need both hands free to concentrate on this puzzle," said Kirsty.

"Why don't you put your other box down too?"

She held her breath. Would the goblin fall for her trick?

"Good idea," said the goblin.

He placed the glass box on top of the snack box and turned back to the puzzle. At once, Alyssa zoomed around behind him and tapped the box with her wand. It melted away, and the rose simply floated into her arms. It shrank to fairy size as she touched it, and a huge smile spread across her face. Rachel and Kirsty shared a hug and jumped up and down in excitement.

"We did it!" said Alyssa, flying across and giving each of them a tiny kiss on the cheek. "Thank you, from the bottom of my heart!"

The fragrant scent of the everlasting rose surrounded them as they smiled at each other.

"Done it!" crowed the goblin, putting his hands on his hips proudly. "See how clever I am?"

He had completed the ice puzzle, and his own face gazed up at him from the puzzle. But as he looked at it, the puzzle face rolled its eyes and shook its head. He frowned, looked up and saw Alyssa holding her rose.

"It's time for you to go home," she said to him. "Tell Jack Frost that my friends and I will never allow him to spoil winter."

She sounded as regal as a queen, and the goblin gulped. Before he could say a word, Alyssa waved her wand and sent him back to Fairyland.

"Now I must take the rose back to where it belongs," she went on, fluttering in front of the girls.

"We'll never forget our amazing adventures with you," said Rachel, smiling at the little fairy.

"Winter will always seem even more magical from now on," Kirsty added.

"I hope so," said Alyssa. "I will never

forget you either. Goodbye, Rachel! Goodbye, Kirsty!"

The girls waved as Alyssa vanished back to her snowy Fairyland home.

"We'd better start walking," said Rachel. "Buttons is waiting for us on the other side of the lake."

They set off arm in arm, and then something beautiful happened. The grey clouds parted, and a shaft of bright winter sunlight broke through. It lit up one of the park's empty flowerbeds, and the girls smiled at each other.

"It's funny," said Kirsty. "The flowerbeds look just the same, but everything is different now that Alyssa has her magical objects back. Now we know that the seeds and bulbs are growing under the soil, and new life is getting ready for springtime."

Rachel nodded.

"Winter is a beautiful season," she said. "But knowing that it will end makes it even more special. Now everyone can enjoy the snowy weather and feel glad that spring is coming too."

"So what do you think is the best thing about winter?" Kirsty asked.

Rachel gave a happy laugh.

"That's easy," she said. "Fairy adventures, of course!"

Now it's time for Kirsty and Rachel to help...

Becky the Best Friend Fairy

Read on for a sneak peek...

The air was filled with the squawks of seagulls and the distant crash of waves on sand. Rachel Walker hopped down the steps of her caravan and grinned. Her best friend, Kirsty Tate, was walking towards her.

"Have you found your caravan?" Rachel called. "I'm so excited that we're both staying at Sunsands all weekend!"

"Me too!" said Kirsty, dashing over and giving Rachel a hug. "Yes, our caravan is just around the corner. I can see the sea out of my bedroom window!"

The girls put their arms around each

other's waists and gazed out at the blue sea. The sun was shining and they were looking forward to a wonderful weekend playing on Sunsands beach.

"Hello, Kirsty," said Mrs Walker, stepping out of the caravan. "Have your parents told you about our plan?"

"No," said Kirsty, feeling excited.

"What plan?" asked Rachel.

Mrs Walker smiled at them.

"There are lots of children staying here this weekend, and we thought it would be fun for you to get to know some of them," she said. "So tomorrow we're going to have a paddling pool party to celebrate new friendships, and you can invite whoever you like."

"That's a great idea!" said Kirsty. "Come on, Rachel, let's go and meet the other children right now!"

The girls darted off along the rows of caravans, looking out for other children. Soon they spotted two girls who looked about the same age as them. One had curly red hair and the other had straight brown hair. They were looking at a book together and giggling.

"Hello!" called Rachel, walking up to them and smiling. "Today's our first day on the caravan site – have you been here long?"

The girls smiled too.

"No, it's our first day as well," said the redhead. "My name's Elsie and this is my best friend Kitty – we're just here for the weekend with my parents."

Rachel and Kirsty introduced themselves.

"What's that book you're looking at?" Kirsty asked.

Kitty picked it up.

"This is what we do together," she said. "It's our stamp collection."

"We love sharing a hobby," said Elsie. "There are some stamps in here that no one else knows we've got."

"It's great to share secrets with your best friend," Rachel agreed, smiling at Kirsty.

She and Kirsty had an amazing secret – they were friends with the fairies, and had often had incredible magical adventures.

"This is our favourite stamp," said Kitty, holding up the book and showing Rachel and Kirsty a small red stamp. "I found it."

"No you didn't," said Elsie, frowning. "I

saw it first!"

She snatched the book from Kitty, who let out a yell.

"Snatching isn't very nice!"

"Especially snatching from your best friend," said Rachel, feeling shocked.

"But Kitty said something that wasn't true," said Kirsty, putting her arm around Elsie's shoulders. "Kitty should say sorry."

Join in the magic online by signing up to the Rainbow Magic fan club!

Meet the fairies, play games and get sneak peeks at the latest books!

There's fairy fun for everyone at

www.rainbowmagicbooks.co.uk

You'll find great activities, competitions, stories and fairy profiles, and also a special newsletter.

Find a fairy with your name!